Nosy Nina

by Suzanne Martinucci
illustrated by Monique Passicot

Harcourt

Orlando   Boston   Dallas   Chicago   San Diego

Visit *The Learning Site!*

www.harcourtschool.com

OK, so I have this nickname. Everybody calls me "Nosy Nina." I like to know things. It's not that I spy on people or anything like that. It's just that when I'm curious about something, I like to check it out.

Take music, for example. I have an older brother, Travis, who plays the trumpet. He takes lessons once a week after school. Sometimes I tag along to the music school and do my homework while I wait for him. Then we both walk home together.

One day I finished my homework faster than usual. Having nothing else to do, I got restless and decided to roam the music school hallways.

The music school is in an old brownstone and has stained-glass windows and a lot of dark wood. I stood in the hallway and listened to the sounds that came from behind the closed classroom doors.

I heard music coming from all over. For the most part, it was piano music. Occasionally, I heard something else, such as drums or a flute. I could definitely hear Travis's trumpet!

Then I heard a different sound. At first I thought it was a person singing a beautiful melody. My curiosity drew me like a magnet to the door where it was coming from. I stood on tiptoe to peek through the window of the practice room door.

I saw a tall girl with two long braids down her back. She was playing a violin. She held the neck of the instrument with her left hand. The other end was tucked under her chin. Her right hand held a long, skinny bow made of wood, which she ran smoothly across the violin strings.

The girl started playing faster and louder. As I watched, I wondered how she managed to get all that sound out of that little instrument.

She turned around and saw me watching her. Feeling a little embarrassed, I wanted to run away. I thought she might feel as if I were spying on her lesson. Then she smiled. She had glasses on, just like me! I wasn't embarrassed anymore, and I flashed a wide smile back at her.

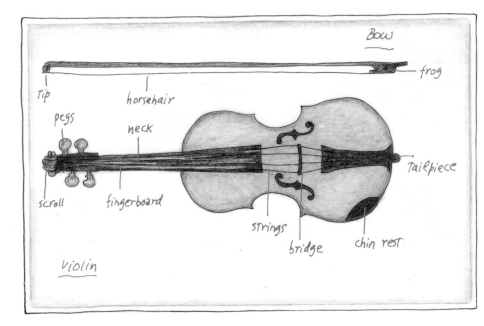

I learned that the girl's name was Tanny. She was thirteen and had been taking violin lessons for four years. That meant that she had started when she was my age! She showed me her violin and bow and pointed out all of their different parts.

Tanny's violin was truly beautiful. It smelled old and mysterious. I asked Tanny about the white dust that I noticed on the wood between the fingerboard and the bridge. "That's rosin," she explained. "You put rosin on the horsehair of the bow to help it move smoothly across the strings."

Then she offered to let me try her violin. Well, all the rosin in the world wasn't going to help my playing. When Tanny played, the violin made sweet sounds. But all it would play for me was "screech, screech!" I must have made an awful face, but she didn't laugh at me. "It's difficult to make a nice sound in the beginning. It takes a lot of practice to learn to play notes," she said.

After Travis finished his trumpet lesson, I could hardly wait to get home. I wanted to ask Mom and Dad whether I could take violin lessons.

I signed up for lessons at the same school as Travis and Tanny. I even studied with Tanny's teacher! Mr. Steele was a great teacher. He began by teaching me how to hold my violin. For the first few months, he tuned the strings at the beginning of each lesson. Then I learned how to tune the violin myself.

I spent many weeks learning how to smoothly bow each violin string. The violin has four strings. The four notes of the violin's "open" strings are G, D, A, and E. Mr. Steele had me recite and hum these notes until I learned them.

A violin's strings are tuned to the notes G, D, A, and E.

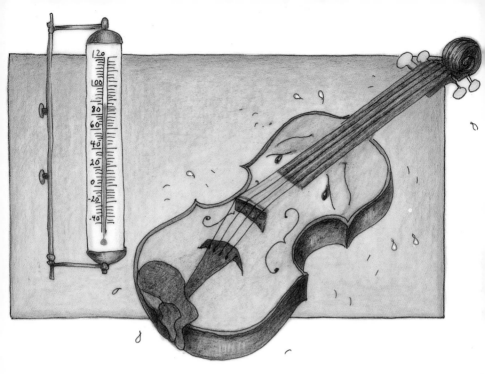

I soon discovered that there wasn't much that was easy about playing the violin. Trying to get a clear sound was hard enough. There was also the problem of playing in tune.

Temperature and humidity can make a perfectly tuned violin go flat. Even when the strings are in tune, you have to listen constantly as you play. On a guitar, there are frets that guide your finger placement. A violin, however, has no frets. You must listen to each note to tell whether your fingers are in the correct spot.

I practiced every day and slowly my playing began to improve. Mr. Steele encouraged me to keep working. He said that if I continued to make good progress, I could perform in the music school's spring recital.

Soon after that, my Aunt Kay dropped by with news of a neighborhood talent show. There were going to be tryouts in a week. I asked Mr. Steele about it, and he suggested a couple of simple melodies that I could play. I replayed them again and again before the big day came.

Well, things didn't go exactly as I had thought they would. At the tryout, all of us were grouped in a big circle in the middle school gym. Then the man in charge went around the circle, and we told him our names and ages.

He asked us how long we had been taking lessons. When I told him "four months," he went right on to the next person. Then he asked a girl to play her accordion. After she had finished, everyone applauded. The rest of us were sent home. I don't think that was quite fair!

Oh, well. Mr. Steele said not to be discouraged. He promised that if I kept up my hard work, I'd play in a recital soon. So, I worked hard at my studies and kept practicing scales and other short pieces. I made practicing fun by pretending I was a famous violinist.

Sometimes Mr. Steele arranged for his students to play pieces together. The first time I did this, Mr. Steele paired me with a boy named Herman. Herman had been born in Germany, and he thought he was really good at playing the violin. We practiced a violin duet while Mr. Steele played the same music on a piano.

Sometimes Herman got a little carried away. I think he preferred to play solo pieces. Mr. Steele would stop us and say, "Now, look at the cover of your music. It says 'for two violins.' When you play a duet, you have to listen to yourself with one ear. You have to listen to your partner with the other ear."

I'm sure this is why Mr. Steele began by having his students play with one other person. Once I had learned to play duets, I graduated to a string group that had four violins, two violas, two cellos, and a bass. To make music with this group, listening was just as important as playing.

One benefit I never expected to get from music was making new friends. That's how it turned out, though.

One day, Aunt Kay came over with another news item. The local children's theater group was planning to perform *The Sound of Music* during summer vacation. They needed people to play in the orchestra. I remembered the talent show that Aunt Kay got me into, so I didn't know whether I wanted a replay of my last tryout.

In the end, I was curious and went to check it out. I ended up really enjoying myself.

The theater group turned out to be a lot of fun! Many of the kids could sing, dance, and act. Others played instruments, like me. Some of the kids didn't perform; they were great at sewing costumes or making scenery.

Our little orchestra must have looked kind of mixed up. I played the only violin. There was also a piano, a flute, a clarinet, a trumpet, and some drums. Playing together with all these instruments was a challenge. Things got even more challenging when people were singing or dancing. I loved every minute!

So, sometimes being nosy can be a good thing! I mean, look at what happened to me. I made lots of new friends and learned a billion new things about music. I learned that sometimes you have to practice something again and again if you want to do it well.

Some people say that curiosity is a matter of "following your nose." In my case, I "followed my ears." After the great time I've had with music, I'd suggest that everyone try following my example.